CW00672330

21 CLASSIC HITS
Playalong *for* Alto Saxophone
RED BOOK

Wise Publications
part of The Music Sales Group
London/New York/Paris/Sydney/Copenhagen/Berlin/Madrid/Tokyo

Published by
Wise Publications
8/9 Frith Street, London W1D 3JB, England.

Exclusive Distributors:
Music Sales Limited
Distribution Centre, Newmarket Road, Bury St. Edmunds,
Suffolk IP33 3YB England.
Music Sales Pty Limited
120 Rothschild Avenue, Rosebery, NSW 2018, Australia.

Order No. AM978318
ISBN 1-84449-214-1
This book © Copyright 2003 by Wise Publications.

Cover photography by George Taylor.
Printed in Malta by Interprint Limited.

CD mastered by Gilles Ruppert.
Instrumental solos by John Whelan.

Your Guarantee of Quality:
As publishers, we strive to produce every book to
the highest commercial standards.
The music has been freshly engraved and the book has been
carefully designed to minimise awkward page turns and
to make playing from it a real pleasure.
Particular care has been given to specifying acid-free, neutral-sized
paper made from pulps which have not been elemental chlorine bleached.
This pulp is from farmed sustainable forests and was
produced with special regard for the environment.
Throughout, the printing and binding have been planned to
ensure a sturdy, attractive publication which should give years of enjoyment.
If your copy fails to meet our high standards,
please inform us and we will gladly replace it.

www.musicsales.com

Saxophone Fingering Chart

LIGATURE

MOUTHPIECE

CROOK

THUMB SUPPORT

BODY

LEFT HAND

1L
2L
3L
1ST FINGER
4L
5L
2ND FINGER
3RD FINGER
6L
7L
8L
9L

OCTAVE KEY

THUMB REST

RIGHT HAND

1R
2R
3R
*4R
1ST FINGER
5R
2ND FINGER
3RD FINGER
6R
7R

THE RING

* Not fitted on some saxophones

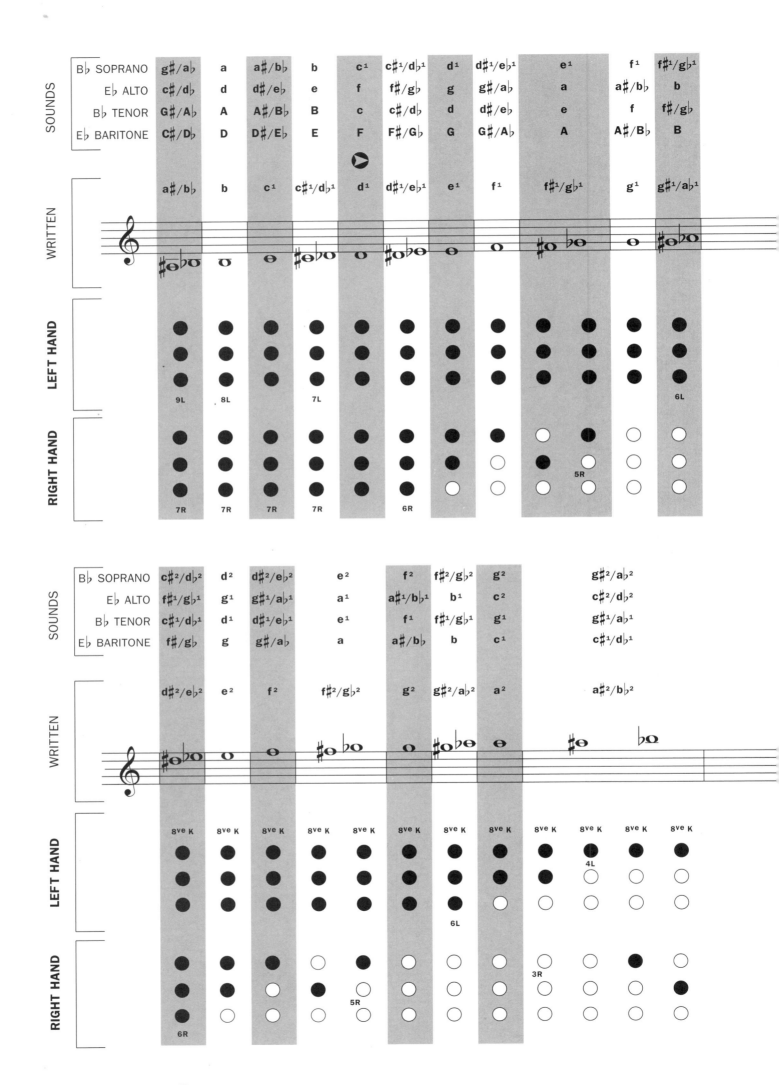

Indicates the lower limit of the best playing range

g¹   g#¹/ab¹   a¹   a#¹/bb¹   b¹   c²
c¹   c#¹/db¹   d¹   d#¹/eb¹   e¹   f¹
g   g#/ab   a   a#/bb   b   c¹
c   c#/db   d   d#/eb   e   f

a¹   a#¹/bb¹   b¹   c²   c#²/db²   d²

4L
3R
2R
8ve K
7L
7R

a²   a#²/bb²   b²   c³   c#³/db³   d³   d#³/eb³
d²   d#²/eb²   e²   f²   f#²/gb²   g²   g#²/ab²
a¹   a#¹/bb¹   b¹   c²   c#²/db²   d²   d#²/eb²
d¹   d#¹/eb¹   e¹   f¹   f#¹/gb¹   g¹   g#¹/ab¹

b²   c³   c#³/db³   d³   d#³/eb³   e³   f³

8ve K

1L
2L
3L
5L
3L
1R
2R

Indicates the upper limit of the best playing range

A Hard Day's Night

Words & Music by John Lennon & Paul McCartney

Slower

8

Come What May

(from *Moulin Rouge!*)

Words & Music by David Baerwald

Steady but appassionato ♩ = 66

(Glock.)

Clair De Lune

(from *Ocean's 11*)

By Claude Debussy

Desert Rose

Words & Music by Sting

Don't Stop Movin'

Words & Music by Simon Ellis, Sheppard Solomon & S Club 7

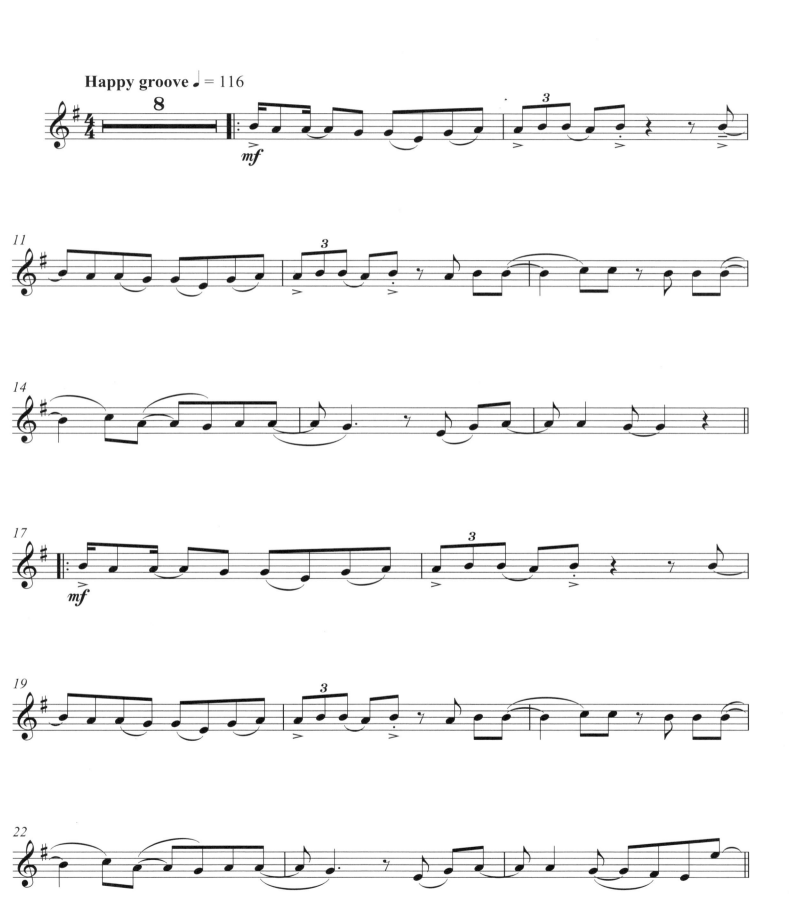

quasi improvised solo

non legato

sub. **ff**

Eternal Flame

Words & Music by Billy Steinberg, Tom Kelly & Susanna Hoffs

Emotion

Words & Music by Barry Gibb & Robin Gibb

Mamma Mia

Words & Music by Benny Andersson, Björn Ulvaeus & Stig Anderson

I Have A Dream

Words & Music by Benny Andersson & Björn Ulvaeus

Natural Blues

Words by Vera Hall
Music by Vera Hall & Moby
'Natural Blues' is based on the song 'Trouble So Hard' (Words & Music by Vera Hall)

Queen Of My Heart

Words & Music by John McLaughlin, Steve Robson, Steve Mac & Wayne Hector

Oops!... I Did It Again

Words & Music by Max Martin & Rami

Passage Of Time / Vianne Sets Up Shop

(from the Miramax Motion Picture *Chocolat*)

By Rachel Portman

PASSAGE OF TIME
Sprightly and balletic ♩ = 90

VIANNE SETS UP SHOP

Pelagia's Song

(from *Captain Corelli's Mandolin*)

By Stephen Warbeck

Pull Yourself Together

(from *Gosford Park*)

By Patrick Doyle

Sail Away

Words & Music by David Gray

The Tide Is High (Get The Feeling)

Words & Music by John Holt, Howard Barrett, Tyrone Evans, Bill Padley & Jem Godfrey

Round Round

Words & Music by Mutya Buena, Keisha Buchanan, Heidi Range,
Brian Higgins, Florian Pfleuger, Felix Stecher, Robin Hoffman & Rino Spadavecchia.

Waterloo

Words & Music by Benny Andersson, Björn Ulvaeus & Stig Anderson

What If

Words & Music by Steve McCutcheon & Wayne Hector

mp *with more urgency*

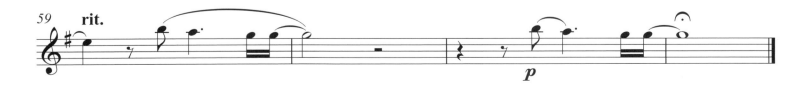

Whenever, Wherever

Words by Shakira & Gloria Estefan
Music by Shakira & Tim Mitchell

CD Track Listing

Disc 1: Full instrumental performances...

1. Tuning notes
2. **A Hard Day's Night**
(Lennon/McCartney) Sony/ATV Music Publishing (UK) Limited
3. **Come What May**
(Baerwald) Rondor Music (London) Limited/EMI Music Publishing.
4. **Clair De Lune**
(Debussy) Dorsey Brothers Music Limited
5. **Desert Rose**
(Sumner/Mami) Steerpike (Overseas) Limited
6. **Don't Stop Movin'**
(Ellis/Solomon/S Club 7) BMG Music Publishing Limited/
Rondor Music (London) Limited/Universal Music Publishing Limited
7. **Eternal Flame**
(Steinberg/Kelly/Hoffs) Sony/ATV Music Publishing (UK) Limited/
Universal Music Publishing Limited
8. **Emotion**
(Gibb/Gibb) BMG Music Publishing Limited
9. **Mamma Mia**
(Andersson/Ulvaeus/Anderson) Bocu Music Limited
10. **I Have A Dream**
(Andersson/Ulvaeus) Bocu Music Limited
11. **Natural Blues**
(Hall/Moby) Carlin Music Corporation/Warner/Chappell Music Limited
12. **Queen Of My Heart**
(McLaughlin/Robson/Mac/Hector) Windswept Music (London) Limited/
Rondor Music (London) Limited/Universal Music Publishing Limited/
Rokstone Music
13. **Oops!... I Did It Again**
(Martin/Rami) Zomba Music Publishers Limited
14. **Passage Of Time/Vianne Sets Up Shop**
(from the Miramax Motion Picture *Chocolat*)
(Portman) Sony/ATV Music Publishing (UK) Limited
15. **Pelagia's Song**
(Warbeck) Universal Music Publishing Limited
16. **Pull Yourself Together**
(from the film *Gosford Park*)
(Doyle) Air-Edel Associates Limited
17. **Sail Away**
(Gray) Chrysalis Music Limited
18. **The Tide Is High (Get The Feeling)**
(Holt/Barrett/Evans/Padley/Godfrey)
The Sparta Florida Music Group Limited/Universal Music Publishing Limited
19. **Round Round**
(Buena/Buchanan/Range/Higgins/Pfleuger/Stecher/Hoffman/Spadavecchia)
Copyright Control/EMI Music Publishing Limited/
Universal Music Publishing Limited/Warner/Chappell Music Limited
20. **Waterloo**
(Andersson/Ulvaeus/Anderson) Bocu Music Limited
21. **What If**
(McCutcheon/Hector) Rokstone Music/Universal Music Publishing Limited
22. **Whenever, Wherever**
(Shakira/Estefan/Mitchell) Sony/ATV Music Publishing (UK) Limited

Disc 2: Backing tracks only...

1. **A Hard Day's Night**
2. **Come What May**
3. **Clair De Lune**
4. **Desert Rose**
5. **Don't Stop Movin'**
6. **Eternal Flame**
7. **Emotion**
8. **Mamma Mia**
9. **I Have A Dream**
10. **Natural Blues**
11. **Queen Of My Heart**
12. **Oops!... I Did It Again**
13. **Passage Of Time/Vianne Sets Up Shop**
14. **Pelagia's Song**
15. **Pull Yourself Together**
16. **Sail Away**
17. **The Tide Is High (Get The Feeling)**
18. **Round Round**
19. **Waterloo**
20. **What If**
21. **Whenever, Wherever**

To remove your CD from the plastic sleeve, lift the small lip on the right to break the perforated flap. Replace the disc after use for convenient storage.